For Theo, who was once a cat — R.L.

Text copyright © Rebecca Lisle 1999
Illustrations copyright © Eleanor Taylor 1999

First published in Great Britain in 1999
by Macdonald Young Books
an imprint of Wayland Publishers Ltd
61 Western Road
Hove
East Sussex
BN3 1JD

Find Macdonald Young Books on the internet at
http://www.myb.co.uk

The right of Rebecca Lisle to be identified as the author
and Eleanor Taylor the illustrator of this Work has been asserted
by them in accordance with the Copyright, Designs and
Patents Act 1988.

Designed and Typeset by Backup Creative Services, Dorset DT10 1DB
Printed in Hong Kong

British Library Cataloguing in Publication Data available

ISBN: 0 7500 2676 6

REBECCA LISLE

Mr Cool Cat

Illustrated by Eleanor Taylor

MACDONALD YOUNG BOOKS

Chapter One

There was a problem at Holly Farm.

Mice.

Mice were everywhere. They were eating through Farmer Meadows' corn and wheat and oats. There were even mice swimming in the vats of milk.

"We should call this Mouse Farm," the farmer grumped.

He had tried everything to get rid of them, everything...

Well, everything except getting a cat... He hadn't tried cats because he hated cats and he hated them for three reasons. First, they made him sneeze and itch.

Second, a cat had once tripped him up
and he had hurt his back badly. Now the
hard work on the farm made his back
ache nearly every day.

And third, he was afraid of them, but he
didn't know why, so he kept that a secret.

But then one day a cat walked right
into the farmyard and sat down by the
kitchen door.

The cat was huge, with marmalade-
coloured stripes and long whiskers.

Farmer Meadows' three children,
Jessica, Thomas and little Ann, loved cats.
They had always longed for a cat.
Cats didn't make *them* sneeze!

Jessica knew straight away that this cat wasn't an ordinary cat.

He was too beautiful. His fur was too smooth. And his nose was too perfect, just like a pink seashell.

"Let's call him Mr Cool Cat," she said.

Farmer Meadows glared at the cat. His back was hurting a lot that day. "Humph," he said.

"Please, please, please can we keep him?" begged the children.

"Humph! Well..."

The farmer looked at his wife.

"Well, all right... but no fussing over him," he warned. "Cows are for milking, pigs are for bacon and cats are for keeping down the mice and nothing more."

"Good," said their mother, "perhaps we'll get something done about those mice at last!"

"And if he trips me up or he doesn't catch mice, out he goes," said the farmer, rubbing his bent and aching back.

Mr Cool Cat lay in the sunlight on Jessica's bed, blinking and purring.

"You can catch mice, can't you?"
she asked, stroking his glistening fur.

But Mr Cool Cat just stretched his legs,
fanned his toes and purred and smiled
and purred.

In the morning the children searched
for signs that Mr Cool Cat had been
doing his job, but they couldn't find
a single dead mouse.

"Perhaps he ate them all up, tail and ears and everything," said Thomas.

"He wouldn't," said little Ann. "He's too nice."

"Humph!" said their father. "Just as I thought. That cat is useless."

"He isn't. He's just kind," said little Ann, "not like you."

"Humph," went Farmer Meadows. He couldn't argue; he didn't feel kind these days.

"I think he's very special," said Jessica. "I bet he can do anything."

"Special! Do anything! Like what? Dance a jig? Juggle with plums?" snorted Farmer Meadows. "All I want him to do is catch mice!"

But the cat didn't catch mice.

Jessica showed Mr Cool Cat pictures of cats pouncing on mice. She pulled a toy mouse past his nose. She even squeaked like a mouse. But Mr Cool Cat lay on his back and showed his fluffy tummy and that was all.

That night, when everyone else was asleep, Jessica heard a noise in the kitchen. Perhaps it was Mr Cool Cat catching mice? She crept downstairs to look.

Chapter Two

Jessica stared. What was Mr Cool Cat doing on the table?

Mr Cool Cat was dancing a lively jig and juggling with six purple plums!

Round and round went the plums, criss-crossing above his pointed ears, spinning and twirling so high they nearly touched the ceiling.

There was one little grey mouse sitting on the dresser watching too, but Jessica didn't notice him, she only had eyes for Mr Cool Cat.

What a clever cat he was!

Jessica blew him a kiss and crept away.

In the morning, Jessica was bursting to tell everyone about their clever cat, but before she could speak, her father, whose back was very bad after the morning's milking, snapped at them:

"Look at this!"

Jessica, Thomas and little Ann stared.

There were mouse droppings on the dresser.

They all looked at Mr Cool Cat as he sat dreaming in the sun, blinking and smiling.

"That cat's got to go if he can't catch mice," said the farmer. "What's he smiling about? He's too well fed. We'll stop his milk."

"But you don't understand!" cried Jessica. "He's so clever…"

"I don't care if he can play the guitar and sing too," said her father. "I just want him to catch mice!"

Late that night Jessica heard strange music coming from downstairs. Was it anything to do with Mr Cool Cat? She crept downstairs and looked in the kitchen.

Yes, there was Mr Cool Cat lying on the table. Beside him was Mrs Meadows' old guitar and he was strumming it with his soft-padded paws. Every now and then he lifted his chin and miaowed tunefully.

Jessica sighed. What a wonderful cat he was!

Jessica was so amazed she never noticed the three little mice sitting on the dresser watching Mr Cool Cat too.

In the morning their parents were very grumbly. There were more mouse droppings in the kitchen and holes in the bread.

"That cat is hopeless!" roared Farmer Meadows.

"But he can play music!" Jessica cried. "He's so clever, he can..." but her father wouldn't listen.

"I don't care what he can do! I don't care if he can skip on one leg on a tight-rope! I don't care!" he said.

"He should catch mice! I'll give him two more days to work out how to do it and then that's that!"

The farmer shuffled out, bent over as if a rock was lodged on his painful back.

"Cats!" he groaned.

Jessica and Thomas and little Ann took Mr Cool Cat into their secret den in the garden and fed him sardines out of a tin.

"Please try and catch a mouse," they begged. "Just a tiny one would do." And they showed him pictures of cats chasing mice to help him.

Chapter Three

That night, when everyone else was asleep, Jessica went down to the kitchen.

Mr Cool Cat was at it again.

This time he was tight-rope walking!

Mr Cool Cat was skipping along the washing line which was stretched from one side of the kitchen to the other.

He held two big wooden spoons to help him balance. What an amazing cat he was!

Jessica watched him going backwards
and forwards and smiled with glee. What
a cat! She didn't notice the five little mice
huddled on the dresser staring. Their eyes
were as round as marbles. They had never
seen anything like it!

Jessica ran back to bed happily.
How lucky they were to have a cat like
Mr Cool Cat.

But their father didn't think so.

"There are more mice than ever," he
complained next day. "What's wrong with
that cat? Why can't he catch mice?"

"He really is clever…" began Jessica, "he can…"

"He can sing and dance and even skate on the kitchen table for all I care," the farmer said crossly. "He's got to catch our mice! Tonight is his last chance, before the mice eat up everything we own!"

"It does seem there are more mice than ever," said Mrs Meadows sadly. "Look! Mouse-prints in the butter!"

Jessica lay in bed worrying about Mr Cool Cat. Surely such a clever cat should be able to catch a few little mice?

When it was very late and she should have been asleep, Jessica crept down to the kitchen and peeped in.

Mr Cool Cat was skating on the kitchen table! As he glided round in a perfect figure of eight, he sang a strange song and juggled with five mouse traps. And that wasn't all, because on his lovely pink nose, he balanced a large piece of cheese.

What a surprising cat he was!

Then Jessica saw the mice. There were mice everywhere. There were mice in the cereal packet and in the jug. There were mice on the shelves, on the table and sitting upon the jam jars.

Every mouse from their farm and all the other nearby farms and fields and hedges had come to watch Mr Cool Cat's final performance.

The mice were goggle-eyed with wonder. They watched Mr Cool Cat going round and round and round... Not an ear flicked or tail twitched: they hardly seemed to breathe.

Now Jessica understood.

It was Mr Cool Cat's plan. A cool plan.

She tiptoed quietly out of the kitchen then dashed up the stairs. She had to tell her parents!

Chapter Four

"Mum! Dad! Wake up! Come and see!
Mr Cool Cat has caught some mice!"

"What! What's this?" Farmer Meadows
sat up in bed and rubbed his eyes. "Did
you wake me up just to tell me that cat
has caught a mouse?"

"Jessica! It's the middle of the night!"
said her mother crossly.

"Yes, yes," Jessica said. "But listen,
Mr Cool Cat has caught all the mice.
There are hundreds in the kitchen!"

Slowly, rubbing his bad back, Farmer
Meadows got out of bed.

"Humph!" he said.

Mrs Meadows got up too and they went down to the kitchen.

Thomas and little Ann had heard the noise and were already there.

"Oh, Dad! It's Mr Cool Cat! You'll never believe how many mice he's caught!" cried Thomas.

"About a million-trillion," said little Ann.

The farmer scowled.

"Show me," he said.

The farmer strode into the kitchen and everyone followed him.

Mr Cool Cat was sitting on a stool. He looked like a king cat. Sitting round the stool was a great crowd of mice, all gazing up at him with wonder.

"Well, what do you know?" Farmer Meadows muttered, rubbing his sore back and sinking into a chair. A smile cracked his face. "What a lot of mice!"

Mr Cool Cat purred loudly, stretched and yawned then suddenly, without any warning, Mr Cool Cat sprang off the stool and leaped on to the farmer's knee.

"Ow!" cried Farmer Meadows, jumping up and throwing the cat off. "Ow! Get that cat out of... here... atishoo!"

He sneezed.

The cat fur had made the farmer sneeze and what a sneeze it was!

It rattled the plates on the table, it rocked the fruit in the fruit bowl and, and...

It snapped the farmer's back, with a crack like thunder.

"Yeow!" he cried as he flew upright, straight as a ruler. "My back!"

He stood still for a moment, rubbing his back. There was no pain. He grinned.

"I can stand up again. Look my dears, I'm standing up straight!"

"And look!" cried little Ann. "Look at Mr Cool Cat!"

He was walking out of the kitchen. The mice gathered quietly behind Mr Cool Cat and followed him out.

The farmer and his wife and the three children followed the cat and the mice to the back door.

"Miaow?" said Mr Cool Cat.

"Shall I open it?" asked Jessica.

"Yes!" said Farmer Meadows.

Outside the moon was shining like a great white dish in the sky. Its silver light gleamed on Mr Cool Cat's coat and glinted on his whiskers. He looked like a magical cat.

Mr Cool Cat walked slowly across the farmyard and the mice followed. They went past the sheds full of corn and wheat, past the stables and past the pig sty to the gate.

There, Mr Cool Cat paused. He looked back at the Meadows family in the doorway and flicked his tail in farewell.

"Goodbye!" called Jessica.

Then Mr Cool Cat and the mice slipped under the gate and set off across the fields towards the dark distant hills.

"That was really cool," said Thomas.

Farmer Meadows laughed.

"I am so happy!" he cried, leaping in the air. "I love cats!"

And the next day he went straight out and bought three kittens, one for Jessica, one for Thomas and one for little Ann. Kittens that would grow up into ordinary, sensible, mouse-catching cats.

"I am so happy!" he yelled to the farmyard and he grabbed some paint and changed the H in Holly Farm to J for Jolly.

"Because that's what we are!" he cried. "Jolly happy!"

Look out for more exciting titles in the Yellow Storybook series:

Sir Garibald and the Damsel in Distress by Marjorie Newman
Sir Garibald's dragon Hot Nose has hatched a new money-making
scheme, turning Sir Garibald unknowingly into a rent-a-knight. But
Hot Nose's plan starts to backfire and one hilarious event leads to
another until neither Sir Garibald nor Hot Nose want to see
another damsel or cat ever again.

Carla's Magic Dancing Boots by Leon Rosselson
Carla loves her new golden boots – they are sparkly and special.
But the next day at school her friends laugh at her. Carla is
unhappy until Grandma shows her that the boots are magic –
magic dancing boots…

The Pony Picnic by Christine Pullein-Thompson
Sophy is really looking forward to the pony picnic. She collects lots
of important things she may need for the trip. But when she gets to
the riding school the other riders, especially her rival Claire, make
fun of her overflowing rucksack. However, by the end of the day
everyone is very grateful indeed that Sophy was so well prepared…

Gorilla Granny by Frank Rogers
Suzie Potts is horrified at the terrible way the animals are treated at
Fred Pepper's Wildlife Park, particularly Gus the Gorilla. So when
Gus escapes and turns up at her back door, she's determined to
take him to the nice animal refuge. But first she must disguise him
and Gus makes a perfect granny.

All these books and many more in the Storybook series can be
purchased from your local bookseller. For more information about
Storybooks, write to: *The Sales Department, Macdonald Young Books,
61 Western Road, Hove, East Sussex BN3 1JD.*